# BILL THE
## and OLD
*by*

## W·HEATH
## ROBINSON

## edited by Timothy Forder

£2·50

Bill loved to wander across the downs. And as he wandered, he would imagine all sorts of extraordinary people, places and things. Unfortunately, he had no one with whom he could share his adventures. 'I rather wish I had a friend,' he thought. So he used to go down to the fields, where he would watch his old Uncle Crispin gather mushrooms. But, gradually, the anxieties connected with mushroom gathering began to affect Old Crispin. 'Oh dear,' thought Bill.

Old Crispin went from bad to worse and eventually he fell ill and completely lost his appetite. Chloe, his wife, called in the doctor, who listened to his chest, took his pulse, and finally sent him away for a holiday.

But it was no use, Old Crispin still wouldn't eat.

With the assistance of Boadicea her daughter, and Chad, her little son, Chloe tried to tempt her husband with every dish she could think of. Old Crispin still wasn't hungry. He became thinner and thinner.

'I wish I wasn't so thin,' he snapped.

Then, at last, Chloe succeeded in making a delicious jelly, that really seemed to take his fancy. And every day she slightly increased the portion. The more of this jelly Crispin ate, the greater his appetite became.

In fact, in due course, Old Crispin spent the whole day eating jelly. He grew so fat he could no longer move. But he still went on eating.

Chloe gave up more and more time to jelly making, until she had to get a minder, so that her children might not be entirely neglected. She sent for her nephew, Bill.

When Old Crispin saw Bill, he said, 'I wish I wasn't so fat.'

But Bill smiled and said quietly, 'I have an idea.'

And he built an amazing slimming appliance, which Crispin had to use twice a day to lose weight. Chloe went on jelly making. And Bill looked after Boadicea and Chad.

## THE KING

One morning, Bill put on his leather waistcoat and filled his pockets with essential items he might need for a trip. Then, he and his companions set off across the downs.

Suddenly they came upon a gold crown protruding from a pile of hay. Slowly the crown began to rise, revealing the head of a king firmly fixed to its underside.

'What do you want?' said the grumpy old monarch.

We wondered why you are hiding out here on the downs,' said Bill.

'If any of you are a bit softish, you had better cover your ears, for my story is a harrowing one,' said the king. And the King told his story.

'I was such a successful king, my kingdom became immensely rich and my subjects worshipped me. Heavier and heavier grew the robes of state until I could hardly support them.

'I was now compelled to remain on my throne day and night. Except, of course, for an hour in the morning, when I performed my ablutions in the royal bathroom.

'My subjects held me in such awe, they would no longer visit me. How I missed the old days – the homely games of dominoes with my ministers; the leisurely cups of tea with my Secretary of State. I was as lonely as a limpet in the Sahara,' said the king.

'One night, after the palace was asleep,' he went on, 'I had a visitor. It was my Prime Minister. "Follow me," he whispered.'

'In silence we traversed the terrace, crossed the tennis lawn, stepped over the rhododendron beds and found ourselves in the kitchen garden. There stood an old hen-house. Inside were my Minister of Education and Secretary of State – playing dominoes. I immediately joined in.

'We caught a plump chicken and cooked it. Suddenly the old cock reminded us that dawn was breaking. And I was hurried back to my throne. Every night was the same. And every morning we were awakened by the old cock.

'One night,' the king continued, 'we met as usual. But to our dismay we discovered that we had eaten all the chickens. Except, of course, for the old cock. After much discussion he went the same way as his companions and we were soon absorbed in our game of dominoes. How long we would have played is impossible to say. For we had eaten our only timepiece. We were suddenly brought to a standstill by a knock at the door.

'My subjects finding my throne vacant had been guided by the sounds of laughter to the hen-house. I was so embarrassed at my appearance, I hurried from my kingdom and I have hidden myself here on the downs ever since.'

Boadicea brushed away the feathers and the droppings from the king's beard and said,

'There, now you can go back to your kingdom.'

The tired old King said,

'I am too tired and old to move.'

'Then we'll take you,' said Bill. And he constructed a wonderful chair, before leaving on the strangest journey Bill had ever dreamed of.

## THE NAVIGATOR

Bill led the way, while Boadicea looked after the old man. Chad plotted their progress on a pocket atlas of the world.

Suddenly the king rang his bell.

'What is it?' asked Bill. And the old sovereign pointed ahead, where a man sat, very still.

Bill approached him and said, 'Who are you, and why are you staring out across the downs?'

'My name is Ron. I'm the navigator on the Swedish liner Turnip of Goteborg,' said the man. 'And I'm looking out for something unusual.'

'Why?' asked Bill.

'For some years,' said Ron, 'I have had my eye on the enchanting Jane Osbaldistone de Trevor of Boulogne, whose father owns a large shipping company. His wealth and importance do not deter me from wanting to marry his delightful daughter. But unfortunately, she finds me dull.'

'Dull?' said Chad.

'Yes,' said Ron. 'Dull and uninteresting. She says I only talk of navigation – of sextants, quadrants, compasses; of logs, charts and tables; of buoys, beacons, knots and currents.'

The old king began to complain of a headache. So Boadicea massaged his temples.

'I understand the problem,' said Bill.

'Luckily,' said Ron, 'my job as navigator aboard the Turnip takes me all around the world. And everywhere I go, I look out for anything extraordinary.

'Have you found anything yet?' asked Bill.

'Yes,' said Ron. And he produced a small brown seed, shaped like a nose.

'What is it?' asked Chad.

'It's the seed of an Australian Nose Plant.'

'Will Jane like it, do you think?' asked Bill.

'It produces the most fascinating flower and the most outrageous perfume you have ever encountered,' said the navigator. 'But it requires ideal conditions to sprout and grow.'

Bill smiled and said thoughtfully, 'I have an idea.' And he built an incredible device for tending the Australian Nose Plant.

But a postcard arrived from the delectable Jane Osbaldistone de Trevor saying that she had married an exciting antiques dealer, who talked of nothing but hallmarks and Chippendale, which spoiled Ron's plans entirely.

Boadicea felt so sorry for him she said, 'We're taking the king back to his kingdom, would you like to come with us?'

'Might as well,' said Ron.

## AUNT GALLADIA

And as they wandered Bill was dreaming about this and that, when he heard the familiar voice of his good Aunt Galladia, calling into a tree. 'How peculiar,' he thought. And the party stopped.

The king rang his bell vigorously, as he was

annoyed at being delayed. So Boadicea poured him a cup
of tea from her thermos flask.

      Bill went up to his good Aunt Galladia and said,
'What's the matter?'

      'I've lost my precious Norris; my beautiful
Norris!' she cried. And she pointed up into the tree.

      There, amid the branches, stood the good Aunt

Galladia's precious Norris – the very rare and beautiful green-toed button crane of Baraboo. In desperation Aunt Galladia tried to entice the animal down from its roost by holding up a Peruvian yap bean, of which the creature was inordinately fond. But the bird stayed in the tree.

Then, with Bill's assistance, she tried to lure the animal from its perch by tying the Peruvian yap bean to the end of a stick. But it wasn't any use. The bird still remained among the branches. And its droppings landed on the king's crown, which displeased him immensely.

'It's hopeless,' moaned the pessimistic Aunt Galladia. 'I'll never get my gorgeous Norris down!'

But Bill pondered over the problem, and in no time contrived an extraordinary device for drawing the magnificent green-toed button crane of Baraboo from its resting place.

'I'm so grateful, young Bill, I want you to keep my darling Norris for yourself.'

'Oh thank you,' said Bill.

'How lovely,' said Boadicea.

'How wonderful,' said Chad.

'How ghastly,' said the king, and he rang his bell impatiently. So they all said goodbye to the good Aunt Galladia, and trudged on across the downs.

# THE RESPECTABLE GENTLEMAN

As Boadicea pushed the King along the path in his wonderful wheelchair, they passed an ice-cream van and he began to grow restless. He greatly desired an ice-cream covered with chocolate sauce. And as they proceeded, he started to show symptoms of becoming a bit unmanageable.

Then, suddenly, they were all greeted by a very respectable gentleman. This man was so respectable, he was never known to wear the same suit twice. Nor had he ever been seen to remove his lavender coloured gloves, even at meal times. It was also reported that his face and inside his ears were never dirty, his hair was never greasy, and he was never known to have to visit the lavatory. He really was a very respectable man.

Then he bowed again and said,
'How can I help you fine people?'
    By now the whimpering old monarch was
becoming impossible to control. He couldn't forget that
ice-cream covered with chocolate sauce. So Bill said,
'Could we have an ice-cream covered with chocolate
sauce for our royal friend?'

'Of course,' said the kind gentleman, and he bowed again. In fact, he went on bowing all the way to the ice-cream van. He even bowed to the litter bin. He really was a ridiculously eccentric sort of person.

When he returned, the king grabbed the ice-cream and sucked it with such enthusiasm, a droplet of chocolate sauce shot from his lips and landed on the respectable gentleman's jacket.

'Oops!' said the king.

'Oh dear,' said Bill. And for a moment the gentleman stared at the ugly brown stain. Then he looked up, and fainted.

Boadicea did her best to remove the blemish with a sheet of toilet tissue. And Chad tried to lick off the blotch

with his tongue. But it wasn't any use. The stain
remained.

So, Bill scratched his head and said to himself, 'I
know.' And he made an ingenious contraption for
removing stains from jackets.

The respectable gentleman was so taken with the

result, he bowed and offered to help the group in any way he could.

'Well,' said Bill. 'It's getting rather late and we are supposed to get the king back to his kingdom.'

'Let me escort the ageing sovereign,' said the gentleman.

And Bill, Boadicea and Chad said goodbye to the king, Ron the navigator, Norris the button crane, and the highly respectable gentleman, and hurried back home across the downs.

Dragon
Grafton Books
A Division of the Collins Publishing Group
8 Grafton Street, London W1X 3LA

Published by Dragon Books

ISBN 0 583 31043 5

Printed and bound in Great Britain by Ancient House Press

Set in Bembo

If you have enjoyed Bill the Minder and want to join
him and his friends helping other children in need – send
your donation to:
The NSPCC, Dept. 68319, 67 Saffron Hill, London EC1N 8RS.